First published in the United States, Great Britain, Canada, Australia, and New Zealand in 2010
by North-South Books Inc., an imprint of NordSüd Verlag AG, CH-8005 Zürich, Switzerland.
Distributed in the United States by North-South Books Inc., New York 10001.

Library of Congress Cataloging-in-Publication Data is available.
ISBN: 978-0-7358-2304-4 (trade edition)
Printed in China by Leo Paper Products Ltd., Heshan, Guangdong, October 2010.
1 3 5 7 9 · 10 8 6 4 2

www.northsouth.com

Pirkko Vainio

Who Hid the Easter Eggs?

NorthSouth
New York / London

It was a beautiful spring day. Harry sat on a branch, swaying in the breeze. He was happy. He could feel the sun warming his fur and smell the fresh green leaves all around him.

Down below, he watched the grandmother walking around her yard. She was carrying a basket full of brightly colored eggs. "It must be Easter!" thought Harry, and he leaped from his branch.

Harry knew that the grandmother always hid painted eggs in her yard at Easter so that her grandchildren could have fun searching for them. He watched her gently place an egg in a hole in the apple tree. She put another in a flowerpot. Harry watched carefully as she hid the eggs all around the yard.

Harry scurried to the apple tree. He wanted
to see one of the Easter eggs close-up. "I've never
seen anything so beautiful." He sighed.
But someone else was taking a keen interest
in the Easter eggs—the jackdaw, Jack!

When the grandmother had hidden all of the eggs, she went back inside the house. Harry climbed up on the window frame to see what she was doing now.

Suddenly he heard a loud *TCHACK TCHACK*. He turned around just in time to see Jack fly through the yard with one of the Easter eggs clutched tightly in his claws.

"Oh, no!" cried Harry. "Jack is stealing the eggs!"

Harry followed Jack to his nest in the big pine tree. And what did he find? Jack had stolen all of the Easter eggs from the garden and had put them in his nest.

Harry didn't know what to do. The children would be so upset when they didn't find any eggs. Maybe Jack didn't know who the eggs belonged to?

"You can't keep these eggs, Jack," said Harry. "They belong to the children."

"But all of the other birds have eggs in their nests in the spring," said Jack. "All except me."

"I'm sure you'll have your own eggs very soon," said Harry.

"Well, if you think so," said Jack.

So Jack and Harry put all of the eggs back in the yard. One by one, they carefully carried them down from the nest, then rolled them across the lawn.

Jack was worried. "I can't remember where I found them all!" he said.

"Oh, no!" Harry sat down to think. "One of them was in the flowerpot," he remembered. "And one was in the apple tree."

Just then they heard voices. The children were here!

Harry and Jack raced around hiding the eggs anywhere they could.

The children ran round and round the yard, but they couldn't find a single egg.

"We're going to have to help them," said Harry.

Jack made a very loud TCHACK TCHACK and flew to the apple tree.

"Look! A jackdaw!" shouted the children. "And there's an Easter egg up there in the apple tree!"

Harry jumped into a teapot and stuck his tail up high.

"A squirrel!" the children shouted. "And another Easter egg!"

Harry and Jack leaped and flew around the garden, showing the children where the eggs were hidden until the eggs had all been found. Then they sat down happily in a tree to watch.

"It's nice to see them having so much fun," said Harry.

"Yes, it is." Jack sighed. "I'd be happy if I found an egg in my nest too."

"Well, maybe I can help you," said Harry.

Harry and Jack went back to Jack's nest in
the pine tree. On a nearby branch sat another
jackdaw with a couple of twigs in her beak.

"This is Jackie," said Harry.

"You can share my nest," said Jack, "if you
haven't already got one of your own."

"That would be very nice," said Jackie.

The spring days got warmer and warmer. One evening, Harry decided to climb up to the top of the pine tree. On his way, he stopped to visit Jack and Jackie.

"Look, Harry!" said Jack proudly. "Look what we've got in our nest!"

There in the nest lay six speckled eggs!

"What a wonderful surprise!" said Harry. "You see. I told you that you'd soon have your own eggs."

Then off he leaped, up to the very top of the tree to enjoy the sunset.